CAROLINE PITCHER has won many awards for her children's books
and teenage novels. *The Snow Whale*, her first picture book with Jackie Morris,
was chosen as one of Child Education's Best Books of 1996 and was followed
by *The Time of the Lion* and *Mariana and the Merchild*. Caroline's latest books
for Frances Lincoln are *Nico's Octopus* and *The Winter Dragon*.

JACKIE MORRIS is a highly acclaimed illustrator whose books include
Ted Hughes' *How the Whale Became*, Sian Lewis' award-winning *Cities in the Sea*
and Susan Summers' *The Greatest Gift*. In addition to her collaborations with
Caroline Pitcher, Jackie has worked with Mary Hoffman on *Parables*, *Miracles* and
Animals of the Bible, and with James Mayhew on *Can You See A Little Bear?*
She wrote and illustrated *The Seal Children* (a story set in a ruined village near
her home in Wales), *The Snow Leopard* and *Tell me a Dragon*.

F
FRANCES LINCOLN
CHILDREN'S BOOKS

Lord
of the Forest

Caroline Pitcher
Illustrated by Jackie Morris

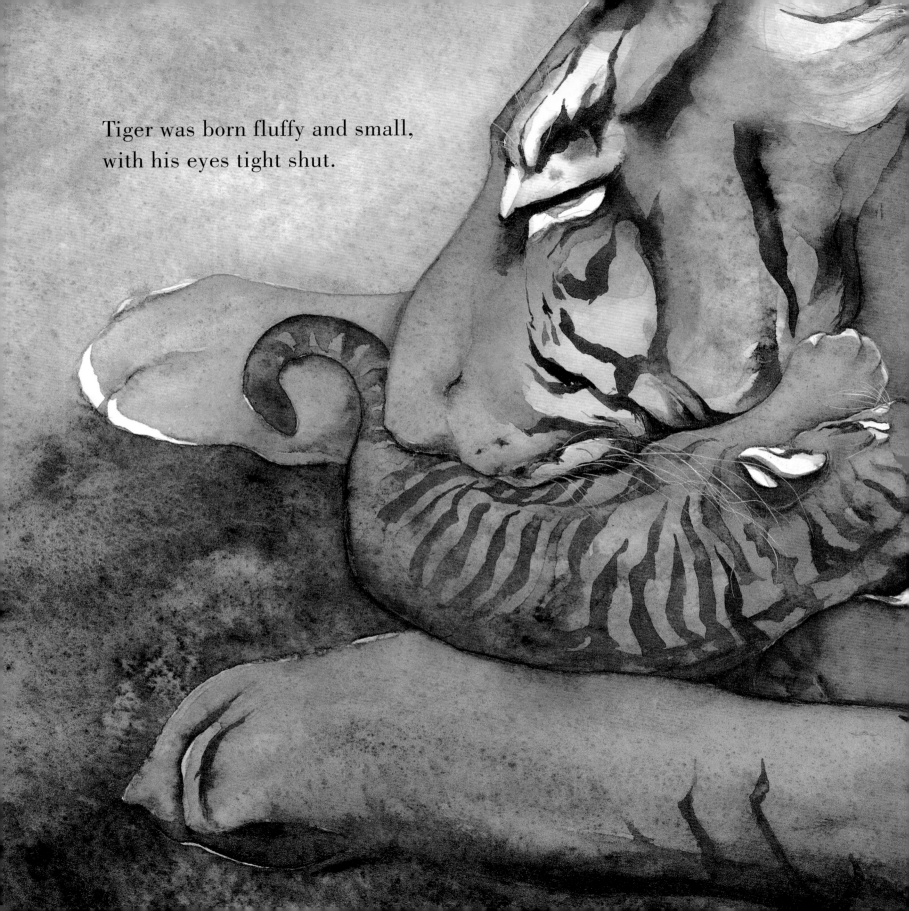

Tiger was born fluffy and small,
with his eyes tight shut.

He twitched his ears and said, "I can hear the forest, the sap rising in the trees and the grass growing long after spring rain!

I hear the slither of zig-zagged snakes and the crow of Jungle Fowl when he wakes.

I hear Monkey whooping to his tribe and the shudder of the branch as he jumps.

I can even hear the curling of Chameleon's tongue and the gulp of little Gekko in the green."

His mother said, "When you don't hear the forest, when silence simmers in the trees, then, my son, be ready.

The Lord of the Forest is on his way!"

Tiger played and fought with his brothers. He swam in the cool water.

He told his mother, "I can hear the creep of crabs from the pool and the flip of fish as they leap in the cool, the croak and splash of jumping frogs and the slither of Water-snake down from the logs."

His mother said, "When you don't hear them, when silence burns and time stands still, then, my son, be ready.

The Lord of the Forest is here!"

Tiger prowled in the mornings when the sun streamed through the mist.

He stalked in the evenings on powerful paws with scimitar claws, and his eyes were worlds of wildness.

When Tiger was grown,
he walked alone.
His shoulder-blades slid
under his golden skin,
rippling through the forest.
He was grass-shadowed and
eye-dazzle bright, a stealthy
cat alone in the night, solitary
cat, with mirrors in his eyes.

Tiger lived his days by lakes
and rocky ridges. He heard
Eagle soaring in the sky and
Ant scuttling down on the earth.

He said, "I am still listening
for that silence, still waiting
for the Lord of the Forest.

Who is the Lord of the Forest?"

"It's me!" screeched Peacock,
strutting with his hens. "I am
lordly, Tiger! Can't you see?
My tail is magnificent!
My feathers are holy.
I kill snakes with my claws!"

Peacock rattled his quills.
His tail with its thousand
feather eyes spangled in
the sun around his tiny head.

Tiger said, "Your tail
is beautiful, Peacock,
but the Lord of the Forest
does not shriek and screech.

Who is the Lord of the Forest?"

"It's me!" roared Rhino, blundering through the trees. "Look at my suit of armour! Look at my deadly horn!"

Tiger said, "Short-sighted Rhino!
The Lord of the Forest does not bellow
and snort and charge like a tank.

Who is the Lord of the Forest?"

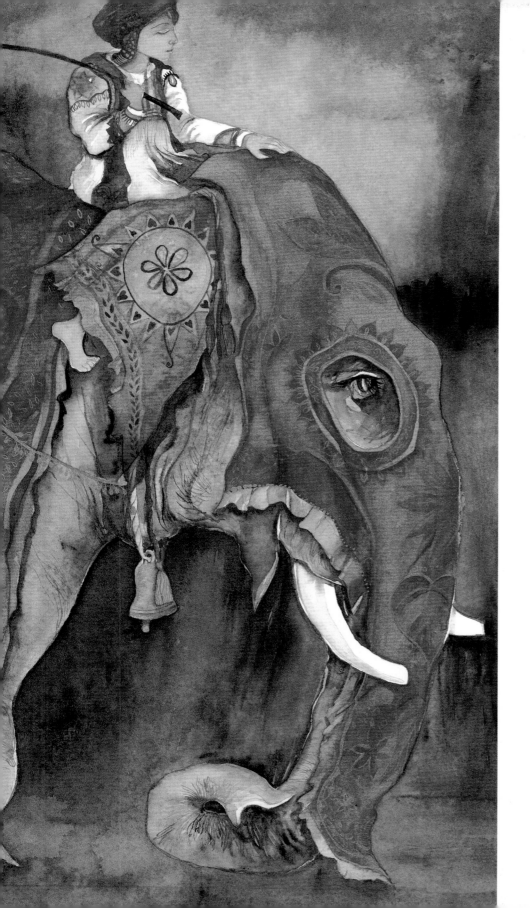

"It's me, of course," trumpeted Elephant, swaying like a ship, his little mahout perched high on his back. "See my tusks gleam! Hear my bells ring!"

Peacock dashed away, shrieking like a cat. Rhino bellowed – and charged into a tree. Elephant stopped short and roared.

"The Lord of the Forest cannot be so noisy," said Tiger. "The Lord of the Forest would never carry people on his back.

Who is the Lord of the Forest?"

Proud Tiger saw a tigress slipping golden
through the grass. He watched the white tips
of her ears and her umbrella-hook tail
held high. Her sides were patterned black,
ferns against the sun.

Tiger and his tigress had cubs, fluffy and small,
with their eyes tight shut. Tiger loved them so!
He licked their faces with his great rough tongue,
nuzzling and purring while he pinned them down.

In the midday heat, Tiger
lounged under the fragrant
mowa tree, as comfortable
as only a cat can be.

He prowled up to his rocky
ridge and stood between
heaven and earth.
He stretched his jaws wide
and roared, "TIGER!"
He stood there still as a statue,
and heard… nothing!
Silence simmered in the trees.
Fear scorched the grass.

"Where are you, Lord of
the Forest?" he roared.
"Show yourself!"

And then the tigress called
him from the pool…

"He's here," she purred.
"Look in the water.

The Lord of the Forest is – you!"

For Joy – C.P.

*For Thomas and Hannah, in the hope that when
your children's children read this book, there will still
be tigers roaming the wild places of the world – J.M.*

Visit the Lord of the Forest website at **www.lordoftheforest.co.uk**
and Caroline Pitcher's website at **www.carolinepitcher.co.uk**

OTHER PICTURE BOOKS IN PAPERBACK
FROM FRANCES LINCOLN CHILDREN'S BOOKS

The Snow Leopard
Jackie Morris

From the beginning of time Snow Leopard has sung the stars to life,
the sun to rise and the moon to wax and wane.
She weaves a song to keep her hidden valley safe
and as she sings, a child dreams her song…

The Winter Dragon
Caroline Pitcher
Illustrated by Sophy Williams

Rory is afraid of Winter's Darkness. He thinks that monsters
and demons might creep out of the shadows. So Rory makes
a Winter Dragon of emerald green, with a crest of brilliant red.

Can You See A Little Bear?
James Mayhew
Illustrated by Jackie Morris

Can you see a little bear hiding in this book? You will see a little bear –
come and take a look. Explore the clues in the nursery rhymes
and sumptuous illustrations to find the little bear!

Frances Lincoln titles are available from all good bookshops.
You can also buy books and find out more about your favourite titles,
authors and illustrators on our website: www.franceslincoln.com